One BiG PAiR OF UNDERWEAR

One Big Pair Of

LAURA
GEHL
WROTE THE
WORDS

UNDERWEAR

TOM
LICHTENHELD
MADE THE
PICTURES

SCHOLASTIC INC.

ONE big pair of underwear.

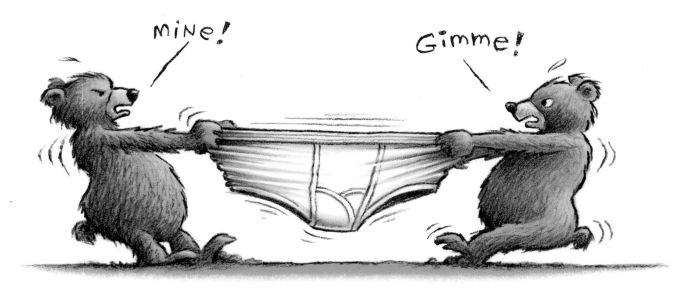

TWO brown bears who hate to share.

ONE bear wears the underwear.

ONE bear cries, "That isn't fair!"

TWO small sacks of salty snacks.

THREE young yaks with black backpacks.

TWO yaks put snacks in their packs.

ONE mad yak yelps, "Where's *my* snack?"

THREE fast scooters, painted teal.

FOUR ball-bouncing silver seals.

THREE seals steal a set of wheels.

ONE seal gets a real bad deal.

FOUR large jars of candy bars.

Greedy goats in FIVE red cars.

FOUR goats gobble all the bars.

ONE goat finds four empty jars.

Pillows sit on FIVE flat mats.

Nap, nap, nap, think SIX fat cats.

FIVE fat cats nap on their mats.

ONE fat cat thinks, Rats! Rats! Rats!

SIX cookbooks in narrow nooks.

SEVEN apron-wearing cooks.

SIX cooks pull books out of nooks.

ONE cook gives them grumpy looks.

SEVEN jet skis, shiny blue.

EIGHT cows craving something new.

SEVEN cows call, "Moo woo-hoo!"

ONE hot cow stews, "Moo boo-hoo!"

EIGHT long sticks and one slick puck.

NINE excited skating ducks.

EIGHT ducks play with sticks and puck.

ONE poor duck is out of luck.

NINE trombones, all gold and grand.

TEN baboons all raise a hand.

NINE baboons march with the band.

ONE baboon gets less than planned.

TEN tall, twisty playground slides.

TWENTY pigs all want a ride.

"Piggyback!" the pigs decide.

TEN pairs glide down side by side.

Bears can see it's fun to share.

They try sharing underwear!

Seals and yaks soon follow suit,
sharing snack packs while they scoot.

Cows, baboons,

and cats and cooks

share their boats, horns, mats, and books.

Goats and ducks share candy bars,
hockey fun, and empty jars.

The friends all share and swap and trade then line up in a long parade.

How did they learn
to count and share?

From ONE big pair of underwear!

The end

For my family, with love—L. G.   **For my dad, in loving memory—T. L.**

ISBN 978-0-545-94074-0

12 11 10 9 8 7 6 5 4 3 2 1   16 17 18 19 20 21

Printed in the U.S.A.   08

This edition first printing, January 2016

Book design by Tom Lichtenheld and Lauren Rille
The text for this book is set in Brandon Grotesque.
The illustrations for this book are rendered in pencil, with digital color and assistance from Kristen Cella.